All of the other alphabet books you've seen have been cute and adorable, I bet. Well, this one is different. This is . . .

OSCAR-THE-GROUCH'S
ALPHABET
OF TRASH

by Jeffrey Moss
illustrated by Sal Murdocca

**FEATURING JIM HENSON'S
SESAME STREET MUPPETS**

A SESAME STREET / GOLDEN PRESS BOOK

Published by Western Publishing Company, Inc. in cooperation with Children's Television Workshop. Copyright © 1977 Children's Television Workshop. Muppet characters © 1977 Muppets, Inc. All rights reserved. Printed in the U.S.A. No part of this book may be reproduced or copied in any form without written permission from the publisher. Oscar-the-Grouch is a trademark of Muppets, Inc. Sesame Street® and the Sesame Street sign are trademarks and service marks of Children's Television Workshop. GOLDEN®, A GOLDEN SHAPE BOOK®, and GOLDEN PRESS® are trademarks of Western Publishing Company, Inc. ISBN 0-307-58013-X ISBN 0-307-68880-1 (lib. bdg.)
B C D E F G H I J

A is for Alphabet.

B is for Busted Balloon.
That's the best kind! Heh, heh!

C is for Can. Here's my rusty can collection. Isn't it beautiful?

D is for Dust. It's time
to dust my furniture.

E is for Eggshells. I always put some in my bed at night to get a crummy night's sleep.

F is for Fishbones, and G is for Garbage. Here's the Garbage Grouch now, with my weekly supply.

H is for Hat. How do you like my horrible hat?

I is for Ice cream. Ice cream is icky—except when it has pickles and sardines on top.

J is for my Junky Jack-in-the-box.
I broke this one when I was
just a little Grouch.

K is for Kite. I fly kites only if I can get them caught in trees.

L is for Ladder. Luckily, the rungs on this ladder are broken, so I can't get my kite down.

M is for Mangled Mirror.
I managed to mash mine in all
the right places.

   N is for my No-good Necktie.
It helped me win the Worst-Dressed
Grouch of the Year award.

   O is for the only good thing
that starts with O—Oscar!

P is for Patched-up Porcupine.
Some people sleep with teddy
bears, but I prefer a porcupine
because it's so prickly.

Q is for Quilt. I've had
this quilt since I was just a
baby Grouch.

R is for Rotten Rubbers that
I sometimes wear in the rain,
which reminds me of my two
favorite S words—Soaked Socks!

T is for Taxi. It's terrific
when one splashes you.
U is for my Ugly Umbrella.

W is for Worm. I now present my pet, Slimey, the wonderful waltzing worm!

Y is for my Yucchy Yellow Yo-Yo.

Z is for Zigzag Zippers. I love old zippers because they're always getting stuck.

There! That's my alphabet of trash—from A to Z! Now, go away!